MORRIS HAS A COLD

Written and illustrated by BERNARD WISEMAN

DODD, MEAD & COMPANY

NEW YORK

For Joe Ann Daly

Graphics Assistant: Susan N. Wiseman

3   4   5   6   7   8   9   10

Library of Congress Cataloging in Publication Data
Wiseman, Bernard.
Morris has a cold.
SUMMARY: Morris the Moose has a cold and
Boris the Bear tries various remedies to cure him.
[1. Sick—Fiction.   2. Humorous stories]
I. Title.
PZ7.W7802Mp   [Fic]   77-12030
ISBN 0-396-07522-3

Morris the Moose said,
"I have a cold.
My nose is walking."

Boris the Bear said,
"You mean
your nose is running."

"No," said Morris.
"My nose is walking.
I only have
a little cold."

Boris said,
"Let me feel your forehead."

Morris said,
"I don't have four heads!"

Boris said,
"I know you don't have four heads.
But this is called your forehead."

Morris said, "That is my ONE head."

"All right," Boris growled.
"Let me feel your one head."

Boris said,
"Your one head feels hot.
That means you are sick.
You need some rest.
You should lie down."

Morris lay down.

"Not HERE!" Boris shouted.
"You are sick.
You must lie down on a bed."

Morris asked, "What is a bed?"

"Well," said Boris,
"a bed has four legs ... "

"Ohhh," Morris said,
"I will not lie down on a bed!
I might get hurt."

Boris asked,
"How can you get hurt
if you lie down on a bed?"

"A bed has legs," said Morris.
"I might fall off the bed
when it jumps or runs."

Boris said,
"Beds do not jump.
Beds do not run.
Beds just stand still."

"Why?" asked Morris.
"Are beds lazy?"

"No!" Boris shouted.
"Beds are not lazy!
Beds are ... Oh, come with me—
I will show you a bed."

"Here we are," said Boris.
"This is the Town Dump.
People leave things here.
We should find a bed here.
Help me look for one.
Look for a thing with four legs."

Morris yelled,
"This has four legs!
I found a bed."

Boris said, "No.
That is not a bed. That is a table.
A bed has four legs, but it is soft."

"I found a bed!" Morris yelled.
"This has four legs, and it is soft."

Boris yelled,
"Put that cat down!
Come here. I found a bed.
Lie down on the bed,
and cover yourself
with these blankets."

"No, no," said Boris
"Do not cover ALL of you."

Morris uncovered his hoofs.

Boris asked, "Why did you
leave your head covered?"

Morris said, "Because
my head has the cold."

Boris said, "Your head
should not be covered."

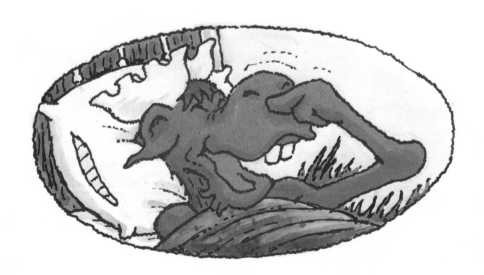

Morris said, "AHH ... AHH ...

… AHH-CHOOO!" Morris sneezed.

Boris covered Morris' head.

"Here," said Boris.
"I found a box of Kleenex.
Pull out the Kleenex, like this.
Blow your nose into the Kleenex."

Boris growled, "You are
pulling out a lot of Kleenex."

Morris said,
"I have a lot of nose."

Morris coughed. Boris asked,
"How does your throat feel?"

Morris said, "Hairy."

"No, no," said Boris.
"I don't mean outside.
How does it feel INSIDE?"

Morris said, "I will see ... "

"No! No! No!" Boris shouted.
"Ohhh—just open your mouth.
Let me look inside."

Boris said,
"You have a sore throat.
I know what is good for it.
I will make you some hot tea."

"Hot what?" asked Morris.

Boris said, "TEA.
Don't you know what tea is?"

"Yes," said Morris.
"I know what it is.
T is a letter, like A, B, C, D ... "

"No! No!" Boris yelled.
"Tea is ... Oh, wait—
I will show you."

"This is tea," said Boris.
"Drink it. It will make
your sore throat feel better."

Morris coughed again.
"Here," said Boris.
"I found a cough drop."

Morris asked, "A cough what?"

Boris said, "Drop."

"No! No!" Boris shouted.
"Put it in your mouth.
It will make your
sore throat feel better."

Boris growled, "You CHEWED it!
You should just suck cough drops."

Morris said, "I am hungry."

"All right," said Boris.
"I will make you something to eat.
But, first, stick out your tongue."

Morris said, "I will not stick out
my tongue. That is not nice."

Boris shouted,
"Stick out your tongue!"

Morris stuck out his tongue.

"STOP!" Boris roared.
"That is not nice!"

Morris said,
"I told you it was not nice."

Boris growled, "That's because
you did it the wrong way.
Look—This is how
to stick out your tongue."

Boris looked at Morris' tongue.
"Oh," Boris said,
"your stomach is upset."

Morris asked, "Did you see
all the way down to my stomach?"

"No," said Boris.
"I did not see all the way
down to your stomach.
I just saw your tongue.
Your tongue is white.
That means your stomach is upset.
I know what you should eat.
I will make you some soup."

"Some what?" asked Morris.

"Soup," said Boris. "Soup is ...
Oh, wait—I will show you."

Boris said, "Here is
a bowl of nice hot soup."

Morris licked the soup.
"No," said Boris.
"Use the spoon."

Morris used the spoon.
"No, no," said Boris.
"Put the spoon in your mouth."

Morris put the spoon
in his mouth.

"No! No! No!" Boris shouted.
"Give me the spoon!"

Boris fed Morris the soup.

Boris ate some soup, too.
Then Boris said,
"It is getting dark.
Go to sleep. If your cold
is better in the morning
I will make you a big breakfast."

"A big what?" Morris asked.

Boris said, "Breakfast.
Breakfast is—Oh! Go to sleep!"

In the morning Morris said,
"My nose is not walking.
My one head is not hot.
My cold is better.
Make me a big breakfast."

"All right," said Boris.
"But you have to do
something for me ... "

Morris asked, "What?"

"DON'T EVER GET SICK AGAIN!"